W9-DEX-084

Into This Night We Are Rising

By Jonathan London · *Illustrated by* G. Brian Karas

Viking

The art was prepared with gouache,
pastels, colored pencils, and collage on
natural fiber papers. Collage images include
photographs and computer-generated art.

VIKING
Published by the Penguin Group
Penguin Books USA Inc., 375 Hudson Street, New York, New York 10014, U.S.A.
Penguin Books Ltd, 27 Wrights Lane, London W8 5TZ, England
Penguin Books Australia Ltd, Ringwood, Victoria, Australia
Penguin Books Canada Ltd, 10 Alcorn Avenue, Toronto, Ontario, Canada M4V 3B2
Penguin Books (N.Z.) Ltd, 182–190 Wairau Road, Auckland 10, New Zealand

Penguin Books Ltd, Registered Offices: Harmondsworth, Middlesex, England

First published in 1993 by Viking, a division of Penguin Books USA Inc.

1 3 5 7 9 10 8 6 4 2

Library of Congress Cataloging-in-Publication Data
London, Jonathan, 1947– Into this night we are rising / by Jonathan London;
illustrated by G. Brian Karas. p. cm.
Summary: Describes a nighttime dream-world where children fly
through the clouds, stuffed animals talk, and stars sing.
ISBN 0-670-84905-7
[1. Night—Fiction. 2. Dreams—Fiction.] I. Karas, G. Brian,
ill. II. Title.
PZ7.L8432In 1993 92-27471 CIP AC

Printed in Hong Kong
Set in 20 point ITC Berkeley Old Style Bold. Title hand lettered by Michele Laporte

For Jeanne Modesitt, Robin Spowart,

and Killarney Clary

with gratitude

For Sean and Aaron, as always

—J.L.

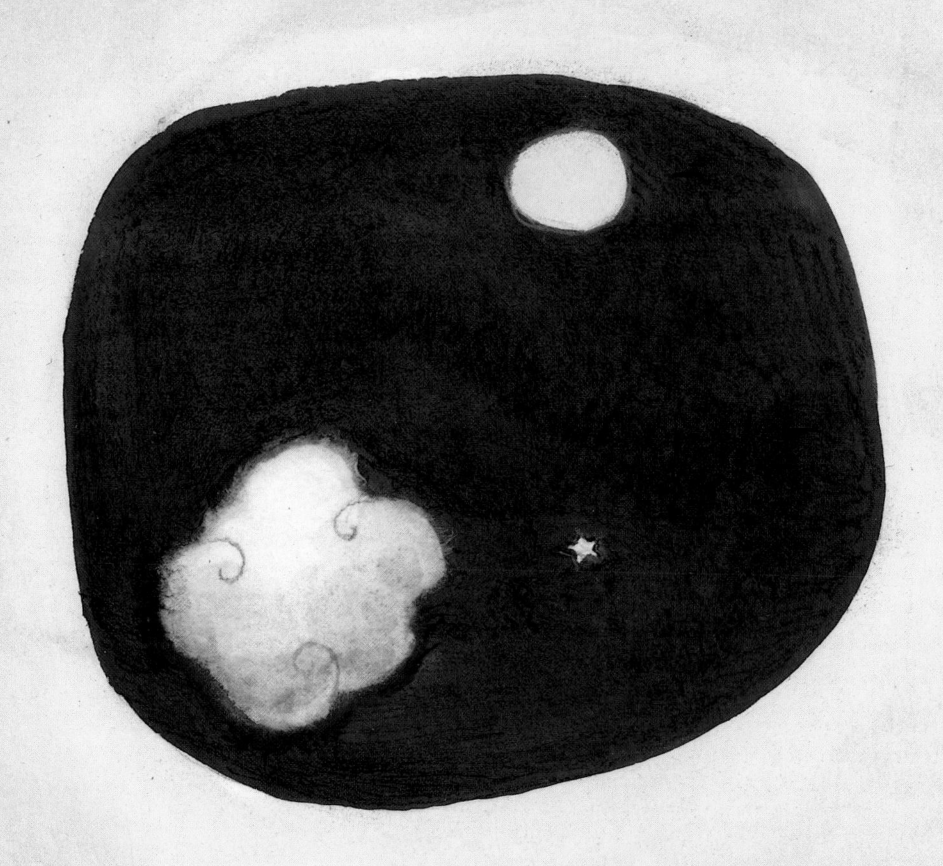

For Sue

—G.B.K.

Into this night we are rising,
leaving our shoes, our toys, and our night-lights.
Out the window we are flying,
leaving our houses behind.

Into this night we are rising
above the villages and towns of the earth.

Pillows of clouds and stars at our feet...
The radiant night is ours.

Pillow fights and children in flight!
We bounce on our beds till they break

and put them back together again
with a sprinkling of dust from the stars.

All our animal friends are here—
our lions and elephants and bears...
They can talk and dance on the air.

The night speaks in so many voices,

and music comes from everywhere.

月

Stars sing their song
and the moon is a gong over China.

Dragons are for riding on here

and there is no word called "fear."

Now down through the night we are falling,
holding hands with all we hold dear.

Down through the wild darkness we are floating
past the giant trees of the earth.

In through the window we are gliding
past the clock ringing its gong.

Back in our beds the day is a flower...
There are petals of soft light in our hair.

What is this song we hear?

Stars sing their song

and the moon is a gong over China…

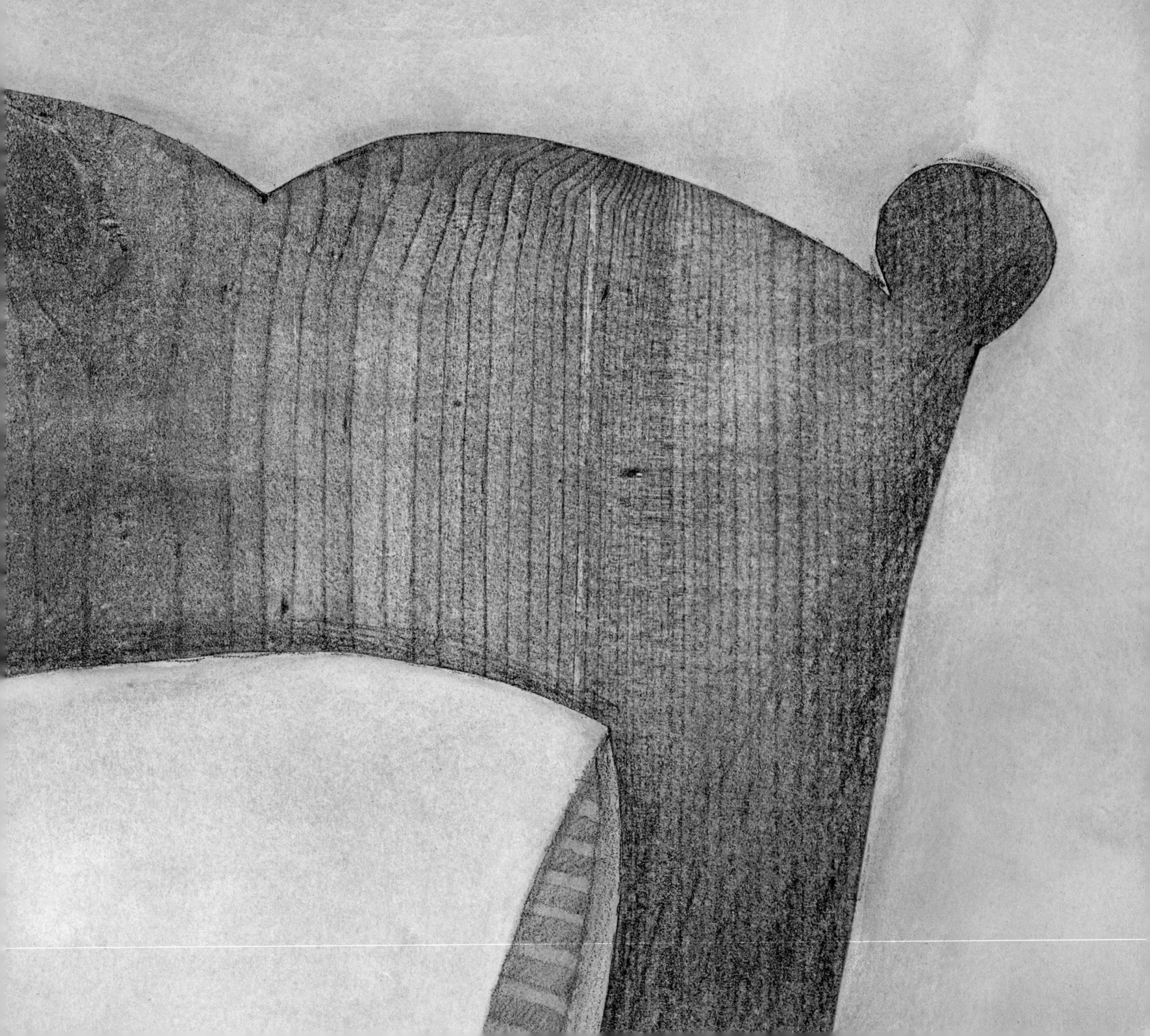

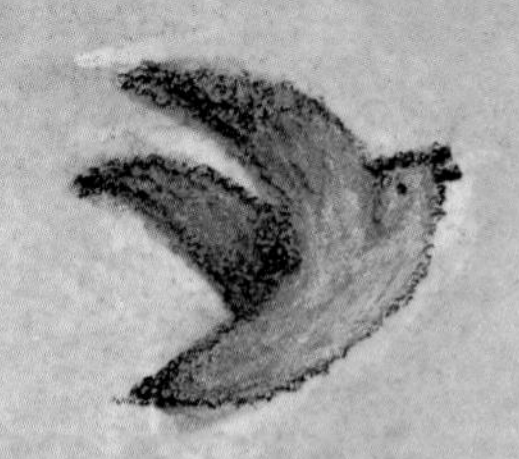

It's the songbird of morning.
Its wings are our dreams

gone sailing...

EDISON TWP. FREE PUBLIC LIBRARY
3 9360 00317141 3